for my Aunt Jess

First published in 1986 by Methuen Children's Books Ltd
11 New Fetter Lane, London EC4P 4EE

Printed in Hong Kong by
South China Printing Co.

British Library Cataloguing in Publication Data

Roberts, Doreen
The Gift.
I. Title
832'.914[J] PZ7

ISBN 0-416-50340-3

The Gift

Doreen Roberts

Methuen Children's Books
London

The boy, Adam, worked the pump handle up and down, up and down, and watched the cool water splash into the old bucket. When the bucket was full it was so heavy that he had to lean a little to balance the weight and some of the water fell over the rim and on to his bare feet. The morning was clear and frosty and Adam shivered a little in his worn waistcoat. He could see the pale early sun glinting far out to sea. A gull screamed overhead, looking for food.

As the boy pushed open the unlatched door of the cottage he could smell the warm temptingness of newly baked bread. Grandmother had just taken a hot loaf from the oven and the sweetness of it made Adam notice his hunger.

He lifted the heavy bucket on to a stool and then on to the table by the window. Carefully he poured the crystal water into the big ewer standing there, then clattered the bucket to its place underneath.

He wiped his hands on a clean cloth and went to his seat at the table. The bread was hot and delicate and the crust crunched between his teeth. The butter sinking into the bread and the milk in the mug beside his plate were Grandmother's wages. Nearly all the food that came into the cottage was given in return for her fine baking and for the sewing, strong and lasting, which she did in what was left of her day.

Grandmother and the boy worked together to grow vegetables and fruit on the small patch of land behind the cottage. There were no flowers because there was no room for luxuries.

Breakfast was eaten in silence. Adam did not speak because he could not, the old woman was silent because she had nothing to say. The boy did not look at her, he knew she was there. She was his security — the gaunt old woman unused to anything, speech or activity, which was not a necessity. She was undemonstrative, but Adam felt her love and care, and the air between them was gentle. He did not think beyond the moment except to wish that he might give her something, something precious and beautiful but of no use but to delight her.

After breakfast he took the crockery to the basin and washed it carefully in hot water which he poured from the big kettle simmering on the stove. When he had finished and everything was back in its place he watched for a moment as Grandmother began to scrub the table. She would not let him do this for her – it was her pride to see the wood white and fresh when she had finished. The boy saw her looking at him and smiled. She nodded and went back to her work.

Outside, the creamy sun had begun to take a little of the frost from the air and a faint delicate blueness covered the sea. Adam stood, looking. He loved the sea, it was forever. It was his life.

The air was still and the boy could see a long way across the estuary, in the silence he could hear faint noises of barges too far out to be visible and a curlew cried away on the saltings. He walked along the sea wall for a long way, there had been no rain and the earth was crunchy and had lost its wet brown-ness.

Down below, on the land side of the wall, a rabbit bobbed its way through the grass and disappeared down a hole as if in panic. The boy stopped and looked and saw a fox running amongst the bushes.

Adam was used to quiet and aloneness, but when he looked back at the tiny group of cottages at the sea's edge, he wondered what it must be like to live in a big town. He wondered whether there would ever be quiet and how people managed to live without the permanence of the sea and the noise of the sea birds. Here, there were not enough cottages to make a real village, and sometimes in a bad winter the sea grew round them and cut them off from the rest of the world. Then they looked like a cluster of stranded birds, huddled together for warmth and protection.

A familiar figure, black against the silvered mud, bent over a wheelbarrow, Jim was collecting winkles. With any luck he would let Grandmother have some and she would cook them ready for their evening meal; she kept special long pins to take the flesh from the shells. Winkle days were treat days and the boy hoped that Jim would have enough to spare. He turned back again and walked on, following the curve of the wall. Around the next bend was his favourite place.

It stood, lonely and austere, dark against the skyline. Once it had been used by the men who had built it – a small rugged church at the edge of the sea. Although the boy could not speak, Grandmother had taught him to read and write – he even had four books of his own, well-worn and well-read for the lack of others. One of them was a history book which told about the men who had come here to this coast, about their lives and beliefs. The boy knew every word of the book by heart and he knew the men in it.

It was when he came to the church that the boy wondered what would happen when Grandmother was no longer there, but the permanence of the sea and the church made it seem impossible that there should ever be a time without Grandmother – and he put the thought from him. He walked round the walls, touching them with his hands and feeling the roughness of the ancient stones.

There was nothing inside the church and the air was chill. The boy stood against the wall and thought of the Grandfather he'd never seen and all the people from times past who must have come to this place.

In his mind he could see them all, the fishermen, the sea-farers, the knights and kings and travellers from foreign places. He stayed inside with them for a while. When he went out the people went too, vanquished by the sunlight and the reality of here and now.

Down on the beach, Adam walked on the pebbles thrown up from the sand. They were cold and hard on his feet but he was used to them.

For a long time he stood motionless, staring at the sea; the sun was warmer now and the whole surface of the water sparkled evenly and gently, the waves too small to break up the softly dancing pattern.

The boy wondered where the sea went, why it stopped where it did and where it came from. The words in his geography book had no meaning, for him the sea was there and no words could bring him a greater reality than this vast expanse. All he knew was that he was suddenly frightened and more alone than he had ever been.

He picked up a pebble and hurled it as far as he could, seeing the splash as it hit the water, making ripples which quarrelled with the natural movement of the waves. He opened his mouth and shouted silently, picking up pebble after pebble and throwing them one after the other until arm ached and fear had gone.

Then he rolled up his trouser legs and ran along the edge of the water, feeling the icy bite of it on his soles. Coming from the sea's rim he trod wet hollows in the sand which dried as he moved on, the footprints following him until he reached the pebbles again.

The boy lay face down, letting the sun warm his back. He scrabbled with his hands and small pebbles ran through his fingers. As he sifted stones, those which had lain covered came to the surface, wet from where the tide had come and gone. He opened his palm and in it, among the browns and the fawns, lay a small piece of deep blue glass; it was smooth, the sharp broken edges honed away by the moving sea. It was very small but very beautiful, like a jewel. The boy put it to one side on a piece of driftwood while he poked about with his fingers, looking for more. But there was nothing. The boy left the glass where it was to mark the place.

When he arrived at the cottage the mid-day meal was on the table – Grand-mother had seen him coming along the sea wall and knew he would be cold. He washed his hands and sat down to eat the steaming goodness. Once more the meal was eaten in silence and once more the boy washed and dried the dishes and put them away.

In the early spring, Adam would work the garden plot on his own, making it ready for planting. He thought about his piece of glass and wished he could go back to the beach, but the light still went very early at this time of year and there was much to be done. When he had finished tidying he chopped more wood for the fire and drew more water from the pump.

Darkness fell very quickly and the air grew cold so that the boy was glad to go into the cottage and sit and read his books until Grandmother had finished her sewing for the day. Adam thought that one day he would try and write down what he felt for her and about the things he saw, but his feelings were too strong so that the task seemed impossible.

There were winkles for supper after all. Grandmother brought the deep dish to the table — it was piled high with the blue-black shells. She smiled as she gave the boy one of the big blanket pins — she knew how their size always amazed him. The winkles were fresh and succulent and tasted of the sea. For Adam, so much came from the sea that he knew that he would find what he wanted there.

The pattern of the boy's life was the same each day. He went to the church and the beach and every day he searched amongst the pebbles. He was patient with his time but impatient in his desires so that when it happened he was taken by surprise.

Searching in the pebbles, his fingers felt something different. He stilled, hardly daring to look.

When he did the depth of the blue made him catch his breath; the glass was twisted and deformed into an unrecognisable shape, but the light caught the surfaces and reflected back the brightness; the edges were smooth and rounded. The glass was as big as the ugly old paperweight which stood on the cottage mantelpiece; the boy could hardly hold it in his cupped hands. He looked at it, laughing silently in happiness.

He put the glass in his shirt, holding it against him in case it should fall out as he ran along the wall back to the cottage. As he burst through the door, Grandmother half rose out of her chair, startled, thinking there must be something wrong to bring him back so early. But when she looked at his face, all she could see was happiness.

They stood facing each other, the boy cupping his treasure with both hands so that she would not see it too soon. He held out his fists at arm's length and thrust them at her so that, instinctively, she put out her hands to receive his gift.

As he opened his fists slowly to let the glass fall, the old woman watched his face and saw the love and hope that he was unable to express in words. She was silent now because she had received his gift before the glass touched her hands.

As she clasped it the boy moved back, watching as he looked down at what her hands held. His eyes followed hers and all the joy went from them. In her palms lay a lump of dead-looking greyish-blue bottle glass. When he had picked it up, the glass had been wet, but now it had dried inside his shirt and the sea-roughened surface no longer reflected the light.

Grandmother knew the ways of the sea, she knew the boy's thoughts and that he wanted to cry and would not. "Wait" she said. The boy watched as the old woman brought out a well used plain glass bowl and filled it with clear fresh water. Then very gently and carefully she put the gift into the water and held the bowl to the light.

The blue glory was back. The late sunlight fell on the glass and the water and the bowl, magnifying and repeating the reflected blues until the whole bowl was glowing and alight with them. She held the bowl between herself and the boy and the wonder of it touched them both.